Little People, BIG DREAMS®
MARY EARPS

Written by
Maria Isabel Sánchez Vegara

Illustrated by
Ana Gomez

Frances Lincoln
Children's Books

In a town near Nottingham, there lived a lively girl called Mary. She loved dancing, swimming, running . . . But her favourite pastime was joining her dad and brother, Joel, for a kickabout.

Mary was ten when she joined her first proper team.
She started as a midfielder but also tried other positions.
One Saturday, while defending the goal, she saved a penalty.
That's when she realized she had a talent for goalkeeping!

Football really changed things for Mary! It made her feel more confident and helped her make friends. At school, she found talking with others easier and was no longer shy about speaking up in class debates.

When Mary was fourteen, Leicester City offered her a place at their training centre for promising players. As she defended her new team's goal, she dreamt of turning pro and playing in the Women's Super League.

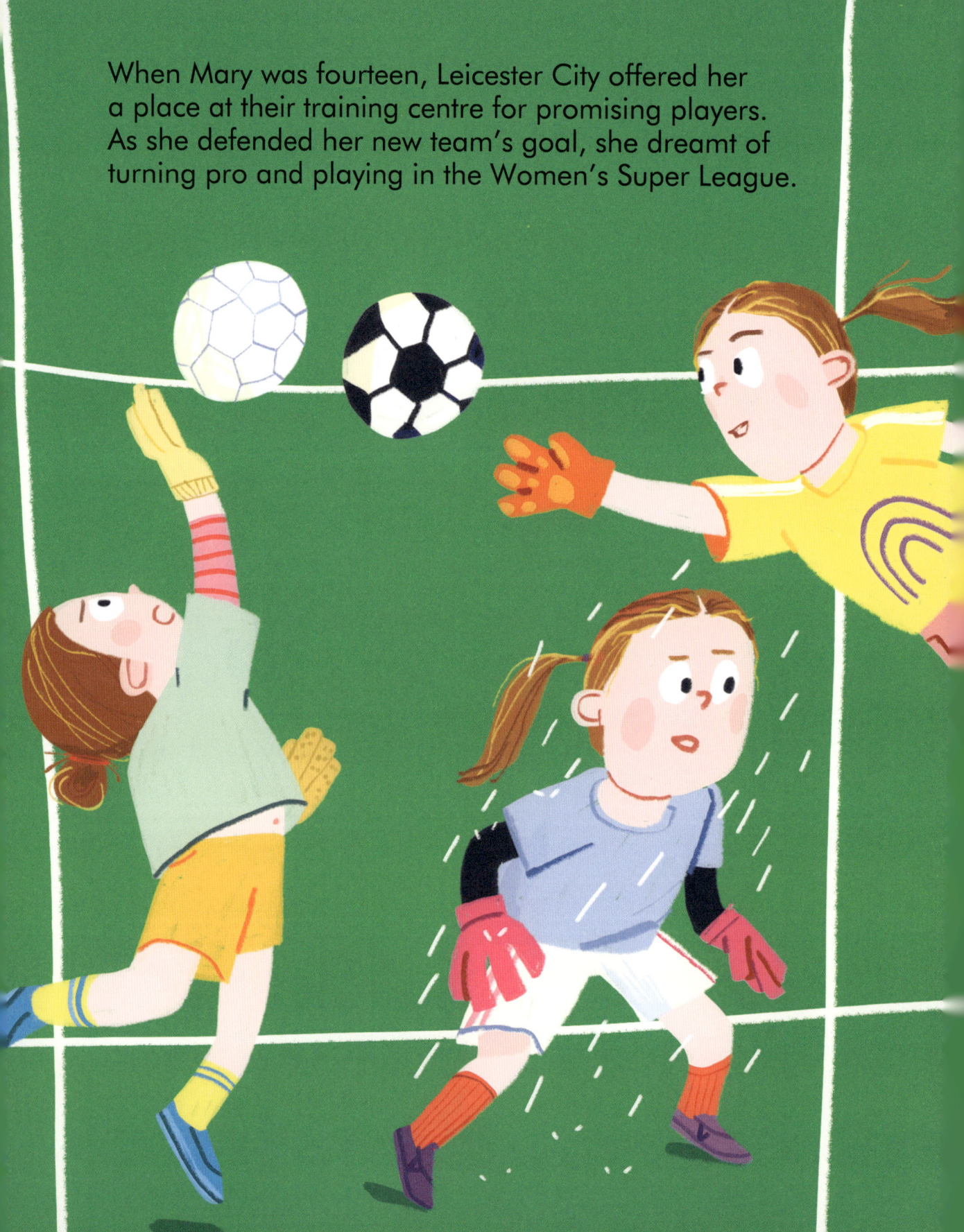

But in England's top women's league, it could take a player a year to earn what a male footballer earned in a week! So, Mary decided it would be safer to go to university in case she had to get a second job to pay the bills.

Upon graduating, Mary made it into England's senior squad, The Lionesses. She was her country's fourth-choice goalkeeper, but that didn't make her family any less proud.

She also proved herself playing for a German team. After Mary helped her club win Germany's top league, Manchester United asked her to be their goalie. Life felt good!

But everything changed when she was suddenly dropped from the England team. To make matters worse, her new contract from Manchester United wouldn't pay enough. Mary thought her football days were over. She had never felt so low!

Luckily, her family and friends were there to pick her up, and her club agreed to raise her wages a little. Then came Sarina Wiegman, the new national coach, who believed in Mary and offered her a chance to play for England again.

A year later, the Lionesses became European Champions! Soon after, Mary and her teammates wrote a letter to the government. They wanted every school in the UK to give girls the same opportunities as boys to play football.

The following summer, thirteen million England fans tuned in to watch Mary save a penalty in the Women's World Cup final in Australia. Although the Lionesses ended up losing, back home they were welcomed as champions.

Mary was voted the world's best goalkeeper, won the BBC Sports Personality award and received a special honour from the Prince of Wales. Everyone wanted to thank her for helping put women's football in the spotlight.

Having become the first goalkeeper to achieve 50 clean sheets in the Women's Super League, Mary decided to leave Manchester United and join Paris Saint-Germain. But she remained a Lioness, always ready to defend the England goal.

And the 'Queen of Stops' has a message for all those who face challenges on the path to their dream:

Sometimes success is not about collecting trophies. It's about waking up and putting one foot in front of the other.

MARY EARPS

(Born 1993)

2011

2017

Born in Nottinghamshire, Mary Earps was eight when she began joining her dad and brother in the garden to play football. Two years later, she joined a local team and quickly realized that she belonged in goal. By 2019, Mary was living her dream, playing for Manchester United and the senior England squad. But her hopes were dashed when she was later dropped from the national team. She became so disheartened that she nearly quit the sport altogether, but her family and friends encouraged her to keep trying. To Mary's delight, a new England coach, Sarina Wiegman, saw her talent and asked her to come back. With Mary defending the goal, the Lionesses won the 2022 European Championship, gaining fans and inspiring many girls to start playing. The public fell in love with Mary's

2022

2024

energy and confidence, giving her the nickname 'Queen of Stops'. Soon after, she was awarded BBC Sports Personality of the Year, FIFA Women's Goalkeeper of the Year, an honorary doctorate and an MBE – and even has a tram named after her in Nottingham! Off the pitch, Mary feels strongly about giving girls and women equal opportunities in sport. She urged the government to add girls' football to the school curriculum and called out a major sponsor for not printing the women's goalkeeper shirt ahead of the 2023 World Cup. When the sponsor finally offered the shirt, it sold out in five minutes! Mary's story reminds us that through the ups and downs we should never stop believing in ourselves. As Mary says: 'There's only one of you in the world and that's more than good enough.'

Want to find out more?

Have a read of these great books:

Earps (Ultimate Football Heroes) by Emily Stead

The Rise of the Lionesses: Incredible Moments from Women's Football by Flo Lloyd-Hughes

To my friend Chelsea, let your light shine bright!

Text © 2025 Maria Isabel Sánchez Vegara. Illustrations © 2025 Ana Gomez.
Original idea of the series by Maria Isabel Sánchez Vegara, published by Alba Editorial, s.l.u.
"Little People, BIG DREAMS" and "Pequeña & Grande" are trademarks of
Alba Editorial s.l.u. and/or Beautifool Couple S.L.
First Published in the UK in 2025 by Frances Lincoln Children's Books, an imprint of The Quarto Group.
1 Triptych Place, London, SE1 9SH, United Kingdom. T 020 7700 6700 www.Quarto.com

All rights reserved.

No part of this publication may be reproduced, stored in a retrieval system, or transmitted, in any form,
or by any means, electrical, mechanical, photocopying, recording or otherwise without the prior written
permission of the publisher or a licence permitting restricted copying.

This book is not authorised, licensed or approved by Mary Earps.
Any faults are the publisher's who will be happy to rectify for future printings.
A catalogue record for this book is available from the British Library.
ISBN 978-1-83600-657-2
Set in Futura BT.

Published by Peter Marley · Edited by Molly Mead
Designed by Sasha Moxon and Izzy Bowman
Production by Robin Boothroyd
Manufactured in Guangdong, China CC012025
1 3 5 7 9 8 6 4 2

Photographic acknowledgements (pages 28-29, from left to right): 1. Mary Earps of Doncaster Rovers Belles FC looks on during the FA Women's Super League match between Chelsea Ladies FC and Doncaster Rovers Belles FC at Tooting & Mitcham United on July 31, 2011 in London, England © Tom Dulat – The FA/The FA Collection via Getty Images. 2. Goalkeeper Mary Earps during an England Women's senior team training session on July 31, 2017 in Utrecht, Netherlands © Catherine Ivill – AMA/Getty Images Sport/Getty Images Europe via Getty Images. 3. England's goalkeeper Mary Earps celebrates on the final whistle in the UEFA Women's Euro 2022 Group A football match between England and Austria at Old Trafford in Manchester, north-west England on July 6, 2022, England won the game 1–0 © Daniel MIHAILESCU/AFP via Getty Images. 4. Mary Earps of Paris Saint-Germain takes a selfie for spectators following the Perth International Football Cup match between West Ham United and Paris Saint-Germain at HBF Park on August 29, 2024 in Perth, Australia © Paul Kane/Stringer/Getty Images AsiaPac via Getty Images.

Scan the QR code for free activity sheets, teachers' notes and more information about the series at www.littlepeoplebigdreams.com